Miss Maclaren

For Lucy May - movie maker extraordinaire
- **Burchett & Vogler**

For Ben Rowland who hopefully won't grow up to be quite as bonkers as his dad x
- **Leighton Noyes**

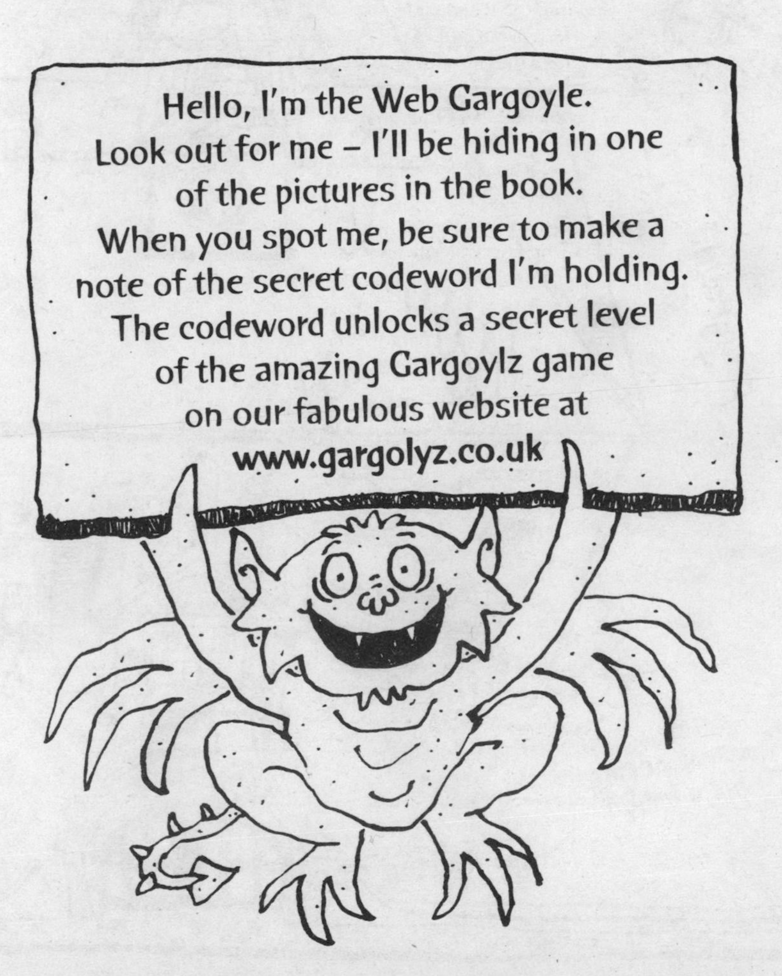

Oldacre Primary School

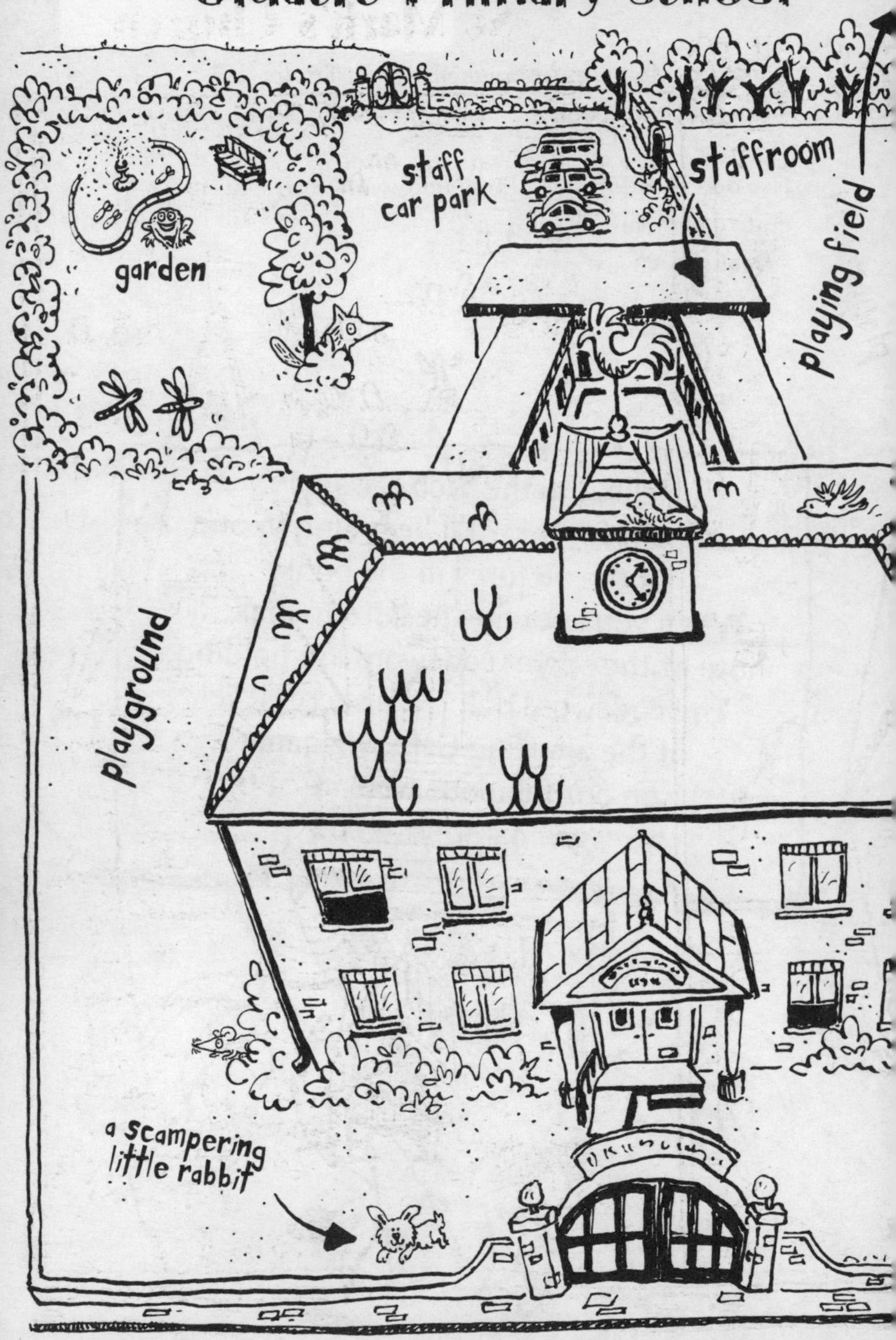

St Mark's Church

School Report - Max Black

Days absent: 0

Days late: 0

Max is never afraid to make a contribution to history lessons. His demonstration of a battering ram using a broom and a bucket was very realistic, although the resulting hole in the classroom door was not ideal.
I worry that Max only seems to play with Ben Neal, but he assures me he has a lot of friends at the local church.

Class teacher - Miss Deirdre Bleet

Max Black's behaviour this term has been outrageous. He has repeatedly broken school rule number 739: boys must not tell 'knock knock' jokes in assembly. He is still playing pranks with Ben Neal. Mrs Pumpkin is absent again after the exploding paint pot incident. And Mrs Simmer, the head dinner lady, says the mincing machine has never been the same since he fed his maths test into it.

Head teacher - Hagatha Hogsbottom (Mrs)

School Report - Ben Neal

Days absent: 0

Days late: 0

This term Ben has
been very inventive in PE.
However, attempting to tightrope-walk
across the hall was a little dangerous
- and used up all the skipping ropes.
He spends far too much time in class
looking out of the window and waving at
the gravestones in the churchyard. He
would be better learning his spellings - a
word he insists on writing as 'spellingz'.

Class teacher - Miss Deirdre Bleet

Ben Neal is always polite, but I am deeply concerned
about his rucksack. It often looks very full - and
not with school books, I am certain. It has sometimes
been seen to wriggle and squirm. I suspect that he
is keeping a pet in there. If so, it is outrageous and
there will be trouble.

Head teacher - Hagatha Hogsbottom (Mrs)

Contents

1. Movie Mayhem

Max Black crept up the path to Ben Neal's house. It was Friday morning and time for school, but first he had an awesome trick to play on his best friend. He pulled a video camera out of his rucksack and flipped up the screen.

Then he pressed Ben's doorbell and jumped into a bush to hide.

The door was flung open and Ben's eager face appeared.

"Hi, Max—" Ben began. Then he stopped. A look of utter bewilderment came over his face. There was no one there.

Trying not to laugh, Max hit the RECORD button. He filmed Ben checking under the welcome mat, sticking his head in the recycling box and searching behind the dustbin.

"Agent Black, Superspy, reporting," Max muttered to the camera. "The Ben monster is on the prowl!" Then he burst out of his hiding place.

Ben yelped in surprise and fell into the hedge. "Cool camera!" he gasped as he struggled out, pulling leaves from his blond hair. "Where did you get it?"

"Dad gave it to me," said Max, hitting the STOP button. "He's got a new one."

"Awesome, Agent Black!" exclaimed Ben. "Let's use it on our spy missions."

"Even better than that, Agent Neal," said Max. "Let's make a movie. It'll be the best movie in the history of best movies – we'll need loads of actors."

"Let's ask the gargoylz to be in it!" suggested Ben.

"Great idea," said Max. "All aboard the spy jet for a supersonic ride to school."

They took off in their imaginary jet fighter and flew down the road towards Oldacre Primary School.

Everyone in Oldacre knew that the church next door to the school was decorated with

gargoyles, but only Max and Ben knew that the little stony statues were alive – and always ready to join in with the boys' tricks and games.

Max and Ben zoomed through the school gates, sped across the playground and came in to land by the churchyard wall.

A pair of small creatures with dragony tails were scrambling over the church roof.

Max brought his spy radar up to full power: cheeky faces, stony skin, mischievous chuckles. He knew what that meant. It was Toby and Azzan, two of their gargoyle friends.

Azzan was crouched down behind the spire and Toby was scampering around searching for him.

"They're playing hide-and-seek," guessed Max. "It's a shame to spoil their fun, but they won't mind when they hear our news." He glanced up and down to check no one was near and then gave a whistle.

Azzan was so excited to see them that he let out a huge flame. Each of the gargoylz had a secret power, and Azzan could breathe fire. Powers like that could be very useful when it came to playing tricks.

But this time the burst of fire gave him away and he was immediately found by his monkey-faced friend, Toby! The two gargoylz scrambled down onto the wall, huge grins on their stony faces.

"Greetingz," said Toby.

Azzan spotted the camera in Max's hand. "Hey, I've seen one of those before. Humanz use them at weddingz. You're not getting married, are you?"

"No way!" exclaimed Max in horror. "We've got a surprise for all you gargoylz. We're going to make a—"

Just then the bell clamoured across the playground.

"We'd better go in to school," said Ben. "Mrs Hogsbottom said she'd be watching us like a hawk after yesterday."

"I don't know why she's making such a fuss," said Max. "We only swapped the caretaker's soap for superglue. Mr Bucket will be able to unstick his hands by next week."

"I hope so," said Ben. "We've got to clean out the smelly old drains for him every break until he can."

"But what's our surprise?" demanded Azzan.

"We'll tell you at lunch time," yelled Max over his shoulder as he and Ben dashed inside.

* * *

"What a boring morning that was," grumbled Max. The boys were bolting down their bangers and mash in the dining hall.

"Mega boring," agreed Ben, "and those drains were super-smelly. The only good bit was when Mr Bucket bent down to do up his shoelace with his hands stuck together and found himself doing a forward roll."

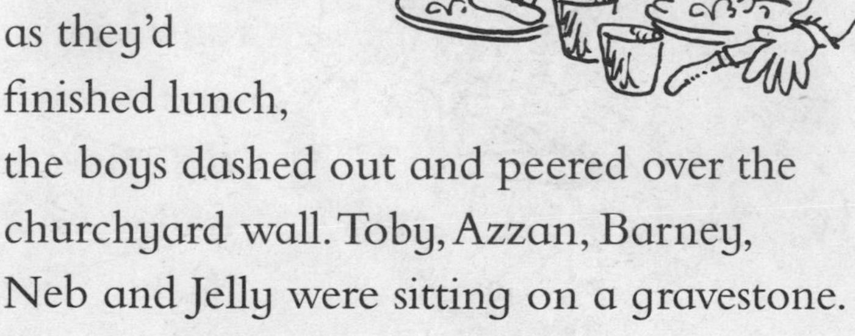

As soon as they'd finished lunch, the boys dashed out and peered over the churchyard wall. Toby, Azzan, Barney, Neb and Jelly were sitting on a gravestone.

"Well?" said Toby. "What's the surprise?"

"Is it cookiez?" demanded Azzan.

"Hope it's cakes," said Neb.

"Even better than that," Max told them. "We're going to make a movie."

"Spluttering gutterz!" exclaimed Toby. "I know all about moviez."

"He's watched enough of them on the television in your bedroom," Azzan told Max.

"I've wanted to be in a movie ever since that TV crew came to film a church service," gasped Barney, shivers of excitement running up and down the spines on his back.

"It was frightfully good fun," said Jelly, flapping his pterodactyl wings happily. "Everyone sang lots of jolly hymnz."

"Until Barney made one of his smellz," chuckled Neb, "and then they ran out screaming."

"But of course we couldn't be in that film," added Azzan sadly, "'cos humanz mustn't know gargoylz are alive."

"You can be in ours," declared Max. "We'll make an exciting action movie. I'll be the director, and Ben and you lot can be the stars."

"**Yippee!**" cried Jelly, and the other gargoylz jumped up and down in excitement.

"I know all about action moviez," said Toby, nodding wisely. "They're always showing those on your television."

"It mustn't be girly," said Azzan.

"Never!" exclaimed Max.

"And no kissing," added Neb, pulling a disgusted face.

"Definitely not!" Ben suddenly looked nervous. "Will there be lots of lines to learn? I sometimes have a tiny bit of trouble with that. Remember the school play when I wanted to be the woodcutter?"

"You didn't get one word right!" snorted Toby.

"You won't have to remember any

words," said Max. "You can make them up as you go along."

"Awesome!" yelled Ben. "Then it *will* be the best movie in the history of best movies. We can all be battling heroes."

"Battling skeletonz!" came a deep voice, and Rufus trundled out from behind a gravestone. The big, warty gargoyle settled himself down beside Toby. "I'll use my secret power to turn into a huge, scary skeleton. It'll be my best performance ever."

"I say, chaps," Jelly piped up. "Why not battling dinosaurz? I could be the fierce pterodactyl."

"Skeletonz!" roared Rufus.

"Dinosaurz!" insisted Jelly, running up and down, squawking excitedly.

"Battling *everything!*" cried Zack, appearing out of thin air with a **pop!**

Jelly was so surprised he melted into a puddle of sloppy purple goo.

"I love it when Jelly uses his secret power," said Ben. "He looks like some weird creature from outer space."

"That's the answer, Agent Neal!" exclaimed Max, his eyes wide with excitement. "We'll make a film about battling aliens!"

"Excellent idea, Agent Black," said Ben. "The gargoylz can use their powers to give us fantastic special effects. We'll call it *Attack of the Alien Gargoylz*."

Ripples ran across the gooey puddle. It bubbled and bulged, and turned into the little pterodactyl again. "Splendid!" Jelly declared.

"Alienz flying and smashing and spying!" yelled Zack, racing up and down the churchyard path.

"Then it's all agreed," said Max. "We'll meet here tomorrow morning to start filming."

The next day Max and Ben arrived at the church straight after breakfast. They zoomed into the churchyard clutching the camera and a clipboard with lots of ideas written on it.

But their path was blocked by a huge pile of dustbin lids, crinkled tin foil and cardboard boxes.

"Who's left all this here?" said Ben. "The churchyard won't look like a scary alien planet with a pile of Earth junk in the way."

"It's not junk!" Jelly flapped out from under a box. "These are our costumes and props for the film!"

Toby flew down from the church porch, tin foil wrapped around his fat tummy. "Greetingz!" he said. "Do you like Ben's astronaut costume? I'm modelling it."

"I'll look great in that," said Ben, impressed.

Pop! Zack appeared on top of the heap. "Dustbin lidz for craterz," he announced, spinning a dustbin lid round on his paw. "You know those holez you get in the ground on the moon? They have lots of them in outer space. We turn the lidz upside down and there you have it – instant craterz."

Barney came waddling round the corner of the church. He was wearing a yogurt pot on his head and carrying a pile of crockery. "We've got lots of flying saucerz," he said, "even if they *are* covered

in painted flowerz. That's because they're the vicar's best ones."

"But they're just ordinary saucers," said Ben.

Suddenly Barney spun one of the plates through the air like a Frisbee, then another. "They're flying saucerz now!" he cried happily.

Max and Ben made emergency goalie dives and caught the plates before they smashed on the path.

"You're right," panted Max. "But they might not last long if you do that."

"It was a good idea though," said Ben, jumping to his feet.

"I know what to do," said Zack, wriggling with excitement. "I'll be invisible and run around with the saucerz."

"Let's get started then," said Max, clapping his hands. "Everyone here?"

Rufus, Azzan and Jelly came scrambling down from the church roof, coat hangers sticking out of their ears.

"We've got proper alien antennae!" explained Jelly.

"I'm here too," said one of the dustbin lids, and Neb slowly appeared on top of it. He'd used his special power to blend in with the background.

"Great," said Max. "We have a star cast and—" He stopped as huge drops of rain began to fall. "Right, everyone into the church!" he yelled. "We'll start our filming in there."

The old wooden doors were open, but as the boys led the charge they heard a ghastly sound from inside.

Max and Ben stopped dead in the porch and the gargoylz piled into the back of them.

"What's going on?" gasped Toby. "Is someone in pain?"

"Worse than that," Ben whispered. "They're singing!"

Another scratchy voice joined in.

"Stay here, everyone," hissed Max.

He poked his head round the door and activated his spy radar: spotty aprons, woolly hats, noses ready to sniff out boys and tell them off. He knew what that meant. It was Enemy Agents Doris and Aggie, codename: Demon Flower Arrangers. The two old ladies had turned on the lights and were sticking carnations into vases on the altar.

Max told his friends the bad news.

"But it's pouring outside," protested

Ben. "We'll have to get rid of them so we can film in there."

Max thought for a moment. "Do you remember Secret Plan: Save Toby From Horrible Old Biddies, when we scared the Demon Flower Arrangers away?"

"It was easy that time," said Ben. "We had a wolf suit."

"Shall I make a smell?" asked Barney eagerly.

"It would certainly scare them away," said Max, "but then we wouldn't want to go in there either!"

Ben's eyes lit up. "Let's tell them the church is haunted," he suggested. "When I give the signal, Toby, you fly up and switch off the lights. Then the rest of you make horrible spooky noises. The Demon Flower Arrangers will be out of there before you can say 'tea cosies'."

The gargoylz nodded eagerly.

"Nice thinking, Agent Neal," said Max. "You and I will go in first."

Doris and Aggie were hobbling up the aisle, still screeching their awful song.

"Excuse me," called Max.

The old ladies whipped round like suspicious weasels.

"What do you want?" cried Doris. "Boys shouldn't come in here on

Saturdays," grumbled Aggie. "They make the place untidy."

"We're on official business," said Max, holding up his camera.

"We're ghost hunters!" explained Ben, waving his clipboard. "There have been reports of strange things happening in this ancient building and we're here to record all paranormal disturbances."

"There's no such things as ghosts," scoffed Doris.

"The vicar would have told us," said Aggie, waggling her basket at the boys. "Come on, Doris. These flowers won't arrange themselves." She screwed up her face and began to sing again.

Max and Ben quickly covered their ears. Ben winked at Toby, who was waiting by the light switch.

Click! The lights went off.

"*Ooohhh!*" screeched Aggie. "What's going on?"

"That was a sign from our first ghostly presence, Mr Neal," said Max in a hushed voice.

Ben scribbled on the clipboard. "First ghostly presence. Noted, Mr Black."

Doris and Aggie looked at each other. "Probably just a power cut, dearie," said Doris.

"Show yourselves, ghosts!" cried Ben in an awestruck voice. "Give us a sign."

For a moment nothing happened, and then an eerie knocking could be heard from the ceiling.

"Spook on the ceiling, Mr Neal," said Max gravely.

"Spook on the ceiling. Noted, Mr Black."

"*Ooh-er!*" wailed Aggie, grabbing Doris's sleeve. "Power cuts don't make that sort of noise."

"It's just the plumbing," whispered Doris. "These old buildings always have noisy plumbing."

"Not in the rafters they don't," croaked Aggie.

At that moment chords of music swelled all around them.

The boys peered through the gloom. The organ keys were moving on their own, just as if a ghost were sitting there playing. The deep, creepy tune echoed around the church.

"Phantom organist, Mr Neal," said Max loudly.

"Phantom organist. Noted, Mr Black."

Aggie clutched Doris by the sleeve. "There's no one playing," she quavered. "It *must* be a ghost."

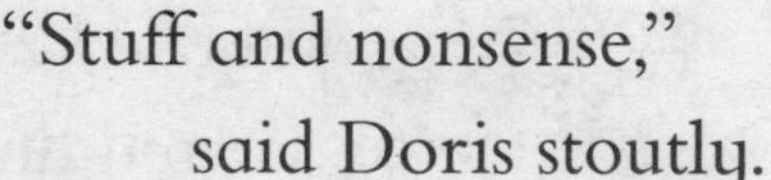

"Stuff and nonsense," said Doris stoutly. "It's probably a mouse jumping on the keys. Anyway, I'm not leaving while it's raining."

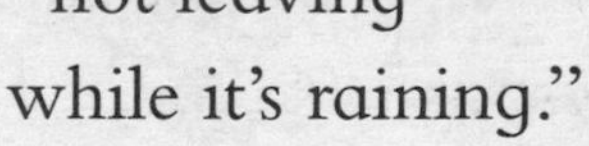

Suddenly the lights snapped back on. A huge skeleton was standing in the pulpit, waving his arms.

"AAAARRRRRGGGHHHH!" The Demon Flower Arrangers fled.

Max and Ben burst out laughing.

"Good old Rufus," said Max. "Just the finishing touch we needed. Well done, gargoylz!"

"Thank you," said Rufus in delight. The gangly skeleton bowed and shrank back into his gargoyle form. Everyone gathered together eagerly.

"Scared the old biddiez!" yelled Zack, running up and down a pew.

"That was great organ playing," Ben told him. "Very spooky."

Zack stopped dead. "Wasn't me," he said. "I can't play the organ."

"Zack was up in the rafterz," added Toby. "He was doing the ghostly knocking."

"Then who was it?" asked Max.

The boys looked at each other in horror.

"There really *was* a ghost!" yelled Ben. "Let's get out of here."

They ran for the door. As they reached the porch, they heard a burst of wheezy laughter.

They spun round. The gargoylz were rolling about in the aisle, clutching their tummies as they chuckled and chortled.

"Tricked you!" called Toby. "There's no ghost."

"It was me playing the organ! I blended with the keyboard," explained Neb.

"That was a fantastic prank," said Max in admiration.

"I haven't laughed so much since Jelly melted on the vicar's duvet and he thought his hot-water bottle had dissolved," wheezed Toby.

"We'll have even more fun in a minute," Ben told them. "The sun's shining again. We can do our filming outside now."

"We didn't need to get rid of the Demon Flower Arrangers after all," said Max.

"But it was super-funny!" said Ben.

Everyone raced for the door excitedly.

"*Attack of the Alien Gargoylz*, here we come!" yelled Max.

2. Enter The Basher

Max, Ben and the gargoylz sat on a tomb making plans and munching on cookies.

"So Ben Magnifico, the space explorer, investigates a strange planet," said Max, scribbling down the plot on his clipboard.

"A strange *misty* planet," said Toby, looking at the steam rising as the sun dried the grass.

"Where he gets attacked by alienz," added Jelly.

"They jump on him," suggested Barney.

"And pull his earz," said Neb.

"And take him to their evil leader,"

put in Azzan.

The gargoylz all talked at once, spraying cookie crumbs as they worked out the plot of their movie.

Ben put on his astronaut's costume – the tin-foil suit, a cereal box with a hole in it for his face as a helmet, and a ray gun made of an empty bottle and a cardboard tube.

Azzan and Neb ran around putting upturned bin lids on the ground.

"That's the craterz done," called Neb.

"Can I join in?" miaowed a voice, and a stripy gargoyle with whiskers came bounding over.

"Of course you can, Theo," answered Max.

"There's always room for another attacking alien."

"I'd have come earlier," purred Theo, "but I don't like the rain." He showed his kitteny claws. "I'll be a fierce alien tiger," he told them. "I'll try not to be too frightening."

Max and Ben grinned at each other. Theo's special power was supposed to be turning into a tiger, but as he was just four hundred and twelve years old – very young for a gargoyle – he could only ever manage a fluffy kitten.

"Attack the astronaut! Attack the astronaut!" chanted Zack. He made a dive for Ben's knees, knocking him backwards into some dandelions. Jelly and Azzan rushed up and started pulling ugly faces at him.

"Not yet!" groaned Ben. "We haven't

started filming!"

"I'll tell you when we're ready to begin," said Max.

"OK, but hurry up," Ben replied, rescuing his helmet from a patch of thistles. "It's hot in this spacesuit. And just attack me one at a time, gargoylz!"

Max held his camera ready. He was just about to press RECORD when Toby popped up in front of the lens.

SECRET CODEWORD:
FILM

"You can't start yet," Toby insisted. "I have to say 'Lights, camera, action' first! That's what proper movie people say. I saw it on your television." He waved a piece of wood with a ruler tied to the top. "I've got my clapperboard. When I click it, you can start the scene."

"OK," Max agreed. "Let's go."

"Hang on!" said Ben suddenly. "I drew a picture of a rocket earlier." He rummaged around in his spacesuit and pulled out a wobbly drawing of something that looked like a fat pencil. "It's not very good though."

"Never mind," said Max. "Jiggle it around when I film it blasting off and it'll look awesome." He looked at the actors. "*Now* are we ready?"

Everyone nodded.

Max raised the video camera again.

"Wait a minute!" said Toby, holding up his clapperboard with TAKE ONE written on it in chalk. "Lights, camera" – he banged the ruler down – "ACTION!"

Max pressed record and focused on Ben's face grinning out of his cereal box.

"It is five hundred years in the future," said Max in a dramatic voiceover, "and Ben Magnifico, bravest astronaut on Earth, is about to embark on the journey of his life. His rocket will travel millions of light years to the planet Splog."

"FIVE . . . FOUR . . . THREE . . . TWO . . . ONE!" everyone shouted as Ben wobbled his rocket picture in front of the camera lens. "BLAST OFF!"

Ben made the rocket rise slowly into the air.

"Let's have some fire, Azzan," whispered Max.

The dragony gargoyle took an enormous breath and sent a blast of flame after it.

"It looks like it's really launching," declared Neb, impressed.

With that, the corner of the paper caught fire and Ben had to jump on it.

"Rocket to base! Rocket to base!" he called in a crackly voice, trying to sound as if he were speaking from deep space. "Fire in the capsule. Going to crash! **Aargghhhh!**"

Azzan took another breath, but this time only managed a tiny flame and a large puff of smoke. Ben emerged, coughing and choking and looking slightly singed.

"Our hero has survived the horrific crash," Max went on, "but what will he find on this hostile planet?"

The camera followed Ben, who was pretending to explore the surface of Splog. Two flowery flying saucers whizzed over his head as invisible Zack ran to and fro. Ben the bold astronaut stalked round the craters, his tin-foil suit crackling loudly. He tapped a statue of an angel on the head.

"They sure have strange rocks on this planet," he said in his best actor's voice, which sounded rather jerky and wooden. He bent down to stare at the grass. "And what's this green stuff? I will test it scientifically." He picked up a handful and put it in his mouth. "Bleugh!"

The camera picked up the sound of muffled gargoyle chuckles as Ben pulled a genuinely horrified face and spat it out.

"Space grass," he croaked. "Deadly poisonous."

Suddenly Max felt a tug on his sleeve and the picture wobbled. He looked down. A bunch of angry gargoylz were gathered around him. Neb was clinging to his arm.

"What's going on?" demanded Max. "You're jogging me." He stopped the recording and played it back.

"Awesome," said Ben, peering at the picture over Max's shoulder. "It looks like a space-quake."

"Never mind space-quakes," said Neb, waggling his nose angrily. "We want to know when we're in the film. After all, we are the starz of the show."

"Well, that would be right now," Max told them. "It's time for the attack of the vicious aliens."

The gargoylz gave a cheer.

"Remember what we agreed," said Ben nervously. "One at a time."

"And don't forget your special powers," added Max, getting ready to film.

"But no smells, Barney," Ben warned.

"Lights, camera, ACTION!" yelled Toby, eagerly banging his clapperboard.

Ben set off round the churchyard

again. Jelly ran up to him, flapping his pterodactyl wings and squawking loudly.

"Oh no!" said Ben woodenly. "A vicious alien. I will destroy it with my ray gun." He pointed the bottle-and-tube gun at Jelly and made laser noises.

"I say," gasped the little dinosaur gargoyle in mock horror. "I've been jolly well zapped." And with that he melted into a gloopy purple puddle.

Then Rufus lumbered up to Ben, growling menacingly. Ben turned the gun on him and his body shrank away, leaving a tall, gangly skeleton in its place. The skeleton tottered dramatically, then fell on its back with its feet in the air.

"Great acting!" whispered Max.

"My best performance ever," said Rufus, jumping up with a clatter of bones, and bowing and waving to the camera.

"You'll have to edit that bit out," said Toby importantly. "I learned all about editing filmz—"

"From watching my television?" asked Max.

"How did you know?" gasped Toby.

"Lucky guess," said Max.

"Now let's get on or it'll be midnight before we've finished!"

"I know all about night filming too," Toby assured him. "We could use spotlights." Then he caught sight of Ben, who was leaning against a grave stone. "No standing around," he called. "ACTION!"

Ben Magnifico made a great show of searching for aliens. "My ray gun's broken," he announced, throwing it aside. "I shall bravely explore without it."

"Who's next on the attack?" whispered Max.

"I am!" chorused the rest of the gargoylz together.

Before Max could stop them they were barging through the tall weeds.

Ben was busy inspecting an alien dandelion when four fierce space gargoylz – and Theo, who was trying to be a fierce space tiger – leaped on him. The heroic astronaut gave a horrified shriek and vanished under a pile of legs, wings and smoke. Zack and Neb appeared and disappeared in turn, while Barney went redder and redder as he struggled to hold in an excited bottom burp.

"It doesn't look good for our hero," said Max into the microphone, trying not to laugh. "He's outnumbered by fierce aliens."

At last Ben struggled out from under the gargoylz. "That wasn't in the story," he groaned, smoothing out his tin foil.

"No, but it looked great!" chuckled Toby. "I haven't had so much fun since

Zack ran round with the vicar's gnomes and he thought they'd come to life."

"Gargoylz, you were awesome!" agreed Max. "There's only one problem. I was laughing so much I couldn't hold the camera steady. We'll have to film it again."

Before Ben could protest Toby scribbled TAKE TWO on his clapperboard and slammed it down hard. "ACTION!" he yelled.

"How many more times will we have to do this?" groaned Ben half an hour later as he crawled out from yet another pile of excited alien gargoylz. "I've had Neb pulling my ears, Barney's tail up my nose and Zack bouncing on my head."

"One more take should do it," called Max.

"Speaking as an expert film maker," said Toby, "that last one looked perfect to me."

"It was," admitted Max, "but I forgot to press RECORD."

"This has to be the last time," grumbled the weary astronaut. "And Azzan – no more breathing fire."

"Are you sure?" said Azzan. "That scorched grass made the attack look more exciting."

"It did," said Ben, rubbing his bottom, "but you scorched me too."

"Places, everyone," ordered Toby. "TAKE SEVENTY-NINE."

This time the filming of the alien attack went smoothly. When Ben the astronaut was completely beaten, the gargoylz jumped up and high-fived.

"What are you doing?" boomed a loud voice, which made them all jump in surprise.

Zack vanished with a **pop!** Neb blended in with a gravestone and the rest of the gargoylz dived into the long grass.

Max's radar burst into life: shaved head, big fists, evil eyes peering over the high wall from his garden, which backed onto the churchyard. Max knew what that meant. It was Enemy Agent Barry Price, also known as The Basher, codename: School Bully.

"We're not up to anything," said Max, slipping the camera behind his back.

"You're hiding something," growled

Barry. "If you don't show me right now I'll come over and see for myself. And why's Ben wrapped up like a roast chicken?"

"We've got to get rid of Barry, Agent Black," Ben whispered to Max.

"But how?" Max whispered back.

"I don't know," answered Ben. "But if he sticks around, the gargoylz won't be able to come out and finish the film."

Ping! An idea jumped into Max's brain. "I've got a great secret plan," he hissed. He produced the camera from behind his back. "We're making a movie," he told The Basher. "And you can be in it!"

"Brilliant!" said Barry.

"I don't call that a great secret plan," Ben muttered.

"We're not having that bully in our film," came Toby's voice from behind the statue of a cherub.

"He's worse than an alien monster," chirped up Neb.

Luckily Barry was too far away to hear them. "I'll have the starring role," he said nastily.

"No he won't!" said Ben through gritted teeth.

"Of course you can have the starring role," said Max. His friends gawped at him in amazement. "As long as you agree to push off – I mean, go and do something else – when we've filmed your bit. We'll show you the movie when it's finished."

The Basher frowned and clenched his huge fists. "No one tells me to push off," he growled menacingly.

Theo gave a yowl of fright from his hiding place and Jelly melted on the spot.

"Wonderful, Barry!" called Max, turning on the camera. "I see you've started acting all ready. That's just what we want!"

Barry turned purple with anger. "Are you making fun of me?" he demanded, heaving himself up onto the wall.

"No, I'm serious!" Max told him nervously, trying not to let the camera shake as he filmed. "The audience won't look at anyone else while you're on screen. You're awesome!"

A toothy grin spread slowly over Barry's face. "I am, aren't I," he agreed, puffing out his chest.

"He's not taking my part, is he?" whispered Ben, horrified.

"Of course not," Max whispered back. "Stop right there, Barry!" he called. "I'll get a last shot of you standing on the churchyard wall."

Barry strutted up and down. "You'd

better show me the movie when it's finished like you promised," he said threateningly, "or else!"

"No problem, Barry," answered Max, hitting the STOP button. "You'll be famous after this performance."

"I'm going to be famous!" exclaimed The Basher. He jumped down into his garden and his footsteps could be heard running towards his house. "Mum!" he yelled. "I'm going to be a famous movie star!"

As soon as the coast was clear the gargoylz crept out of their hiding places.

"Is that bully really going to be in our movie?" asked Neb in disgust.

"Yes," said Max firmly. "But he's not going to be the hero like he thinks. My voiceover's going to turn him into an evil alien!"

"That's a relief," said Ben.

Max rewound to the image of the gargoylz piled on top of Ben and began his voiceover: "After the attack by the army of strange creatures, there was worse to come. Our brave hero was about to meet the ugliest and stinkiest of all the monsters – the terrible beast that lived on top of the highest mountain on Splog – Barry the Bashgroozle!"

The Basher came up on the screen. He was purple in the face, waving his fists about and snarling menacingly. The gargoylz burst out laughing.

When Barry's scene had finished, Max hit STOP. "Ben, I want you to pretend you've just spotted the Bashgroozle and you're sick with terror."

"LIGHTS, CAMERA, ACTION!" yelled Toby, deafening everyone with his clapperboard.

Max filmed a close-up of the astronaut, who was pulling a face as if he'd got toffee stuck in his teeth.

"You look like a demented camel!" declared Max. "Think of something really scary – like being given extra homework."

"It's no better," sighed Azzan as Ben tried to make his knees knock together.

"Is he dancing?" asked Jelly. "It's very jolly."

"He needs help," said Barney firmly. "My special power should do the trick – a nice smelly bottom burp."

A glazed look came over the little gargoyle's doggy face, and the next minute the most dreadful pong filled the air.

"It's horrible!" spluttered Ben, turning green. "I can't breathe!"

The gargoylz backed off, fanning the air with wings and tails while Ben staggered about, gasping for breath.

"Perfect!" called Max, filming Ben as he collapsed on the ground. "Very realistic."

"Barry the Bashgroozle has defeated the space traveller," declared Rufus, stepping into the shot and looming over Ben Magnifico. "We shall take him to our leader."

The gargoylz dragged the helpless astronaut away by his boots.

"What will happen to our brave hero?" said Max into the camera. "Could this be his final mission? Is this THE END for Ben Magnifico?"

"AND CUT!" yelled Toby. "Dangling

drainpipes! This is going to be better than some of those moviez I've seen on y—"

But he was knocked aside by his stony friends scampering up to surround Max. They looked worried.

"What will happen?" whispered Barney.

"Could this be his final mission?" asked Theo.

"Is it really THE END of our brave hero?" demanded Rufus.

"Tell us!" said Neb anxiously.

Max grinned. "Ben and I have got to go home now," he said. "But you'll find out tomorrow morning."

3. Movie Magic

It was Sunday morning. Max, Ben and the gargoylz were back in the churchyard filming the very last scene of their movie.

"Goodbye, Ben Magnifico!" sobbed the alien gargoylz, getting out their alien hankies and dabbing their alien eyes. "We will be friendz for ever."

Ben strapped on his super astronaut jet pack – two washing-up bottles in tin foil – and took off for the stars.

"And that's a wrap!" called Max, hitting the STOP button for the last time.

"That means the film is finished,"

put in Toby importantly.

"I'm so glad the brave space explorer made peace with the alienz," purred Theo. "I love a happy ending."

"It was jolly clever when Ben Magnifico told them to eat cupcakes instead of him," beamed Jelly.

"And they were delicious!" said Barney, licking his lips.

"I didn't want it to end," said Azzan, his dragony tail drooping.

"It's not over." Max gave a huge grin. "We've got to watch our movie now."

The gargoylz cheered.

"We'll meet you in my bedroom in twenty minutes for a special screening," Max went on.

"We'll be there before you!" shouted Toby.

And with a **whoosh**, the little creatures scuttled into the long grass.

"Spy hovercraft ready to launch!" yelled Max as they set off on Ben's skateboard. They dodged between people coming to church for the Sunday-morning service.

"Enemy agents ahead!" gasped Ben.

Max turned on his spy radar: Sunday-best flowery coats, Sunday-best woolly

hats, Sunday-best spotty rainhoods. He knew what that meant. It was Enemy Agents Doris and Aggie, codename: Demon Flower Arrangers. They were on their way to St Mark's – on a collision course with the boys.

"We need a Superspy hiding place, Agent Neal," yelled Max.

Ben steered the hovercraft behind a tall gravestone just as the two old biddies came along. Aggie stopped dead and rummaged in her bag.

"I'm making sure I've got my Sunday-best hankie," she croaked, glancing nervously at the church.

"No you're not, Aggie," snapped Doris. "You're scared to go in because of that ghost organist."

"So are you," insisted her friend.

"Don't be silly," said Doris indignantly.

"You go first then," said Aggie.

Doris gulped and grasped her friend's arm. "Let's go together, Aggie dear. And I'm going to give that vicar a piece of my mind. He should have told us about the ghost."

"A rousing song will help us on our way," said Aggie, beginning to warble another old song that Max and Ben had never heard of.

Doris joined in, grim faced and they began to shuffle off down the path.

"Should we tell them there wasn't a ghost?" whispered Ben.

"No!" replied Max. "We're doing them a favour. They love moaning and we've given them something new to moan about."

They sped off again.

"We must have broken the world record for speedy hovercrafting," yelled Ben as they swerved expertly down Max's garden path.

"Careful, boys!"

It was Mrs Black. She was coming out of the front door, followed by Jessica, Max's annoying little sister.

"Yes, boys," said Jessica, putting on

a silly grown-up voice. "Be careful!"

Ben skilfully brought the skateboard to a screeching halt and they both fell off.

"We're going to the cinema," Mum told them. "That new animated pony film's on. I expect you'd like to come."

Max and Ben leaped to their feet, looking horrified.

"Normally we'd love to," said Ben.

"But we're super busy," Max added, holding up the video camera. "We've got our own film to watch."

"You won't get any popcorn if you don't come," chanted Jessica.

"They can have popcorn too," said Mrs Black. "Your dad's in the garden, Max. He'll make you some. Then it'll be exactly like the cinema."

Jessica scowled and marched off to the car.

"Awesome!" shouted Ben. "Your dad makes the best popcorn in the history of best popcorn!"

They ran down the side path into the garden.

Dad was kneeling by a flowerbed, his tongue sticking out as he carefully tied up his tomato plants.

The boys took it in turns to tell him about their movie, making sure they didn't mention their gargoyle friends.

"So you see," finished Max, "we've worked so hard, and now our reward is to watch our film. Mum said you'd make us some popcorn."

"Popcorn coming up," said Dad cheerfully. "You plug your camera into the big TV in the lounge and we'll all watch your movie together."

"Er, we'd love to do that . . ." said Max, speaking slowly and thinking fast.

"But this is the special director's cut," he finished triumphantly.

"That's right," added Ben. "It'll need a lot of editing. We can only show it to the public when it's perfect."

"You sound like proper film makers," chuckled Dad, setting off for the kitchen. "OK, I'll stay away until it's ready. I'll leave the popcorn in the lounge for you."

"Thanks, Dad," said Max. "You can be our official film caterer."

They dashed upstairs and burst into Max's bedroom.

The gargoylz were all there, tucked up under the duvet, watching a programme about meerkats.

"Good news!" announced Max. "We're going to watch our movie on the big screen downstairs – with a special snack."

The gargoylz cheered enthusiastically.

"We just have to wait till Dad's gone back outside—" Max stopped and gulped. "I'll brave the nasty clean flowery smell in my sister's bedroom. You can see the whole garden from her window."

"Can you hold your breath that long?" asked Toby, a look of concern on his face.

Max nodded grimly and set off on his dangerous mission. A few moments later he was back, gasping for air. "Dad's got his head in the compost," he panted. "It's safe to go into the lounge!"

They all charged downstairs and flung themselves on the sofa. Max grabbed the remote control while the gargoylz dived into the huge bowl of sticky golden popcorn on the coffee table. The film started.

The audience whooped as the alien gargoylz appeared and attacked Ben Magnifico.

"This is awesome!" gasped Ben. "We'll all win Oscars."

"What's an Oscar?" demanded Theo.

"Can you eat it?" asked Barney.

"It's a statue of a man that they give to the best film actors in the world," Max told them.

"I deserve one of those," said Rufus, puffing out his chest. "See the way my bones are shining menacingly in the light."

"And that's the best bit of alien melting I've ever done," declared Jelly.

"And I'll win one for making the hottest fire ever when the rocket took off," added Azzan, snorting a burst of flame.

Max moved the remote control away from the gargoyle just in time. "They don't give Oscars for melting vital bits of equipment!" he exclaimed.

"Shhh!" said Barney. "We're just coming to the bit where we all jump on Ben Magnifico."

"I did some particularly clever clapperboarding in that part!" said Toby. "I haven't had so much fun since Barney painted the vicar's microwave yellow and he thought his custard had exploded."

"Our alien attack was the best bit of the film," agreed Neb.

"It was the *worst* bit for me," groaned Ben. "I've still got the bruises!"

BANG!

"That was the front door," said Max in horror.

Running footsteps could be heard in the hall and a shrill voice shouted, "Ice-cream time!"

Max activated his spy radar: small, shriekingly loud and coming their way. He knew what that meant. It was Enemy Agent Jessica Black, codename: Disgusting Little Sister.

"Spluttering gutterz!" cried Toby in alarm. "We'd better hide."

The lounge door was beginning to open. **Pop!** Zack went invisible and Neb

blended with the curtains. The other gargoylz dived into the tiny space behind the sofa. And just in time.

"Is this your movie?" demanded Jessica, running up to the television.

Max fumbled for the remote control to stop the film but he was too late. Jessica snatched it up.

"Mum!" she screeched. "Dad! Come and see Max's movie."

Max made a grab for the remote but she stuffed it up her jumper.

"The film's ready, is it?" said Dad, following Mum eagerly into the room.

"No!" yelled Max, leaping in front of the screen.

"You're just being modest," said Mum as Jessica shoved him aside. "It looks very interesting."

Max's family plonked themselves down on the sofa and began to watch as a tin-foil-covered figure with a box on his head appeared on the screen.

"That's Ben!" shrilled Jessica. "He looks stupid."

"Don't be mean, Jess," protested her mum. "He's a very realistic – er . . ."

"Astronaut," said Ben.

"Astronaut," said Mrs Black.

"Oh, it's a space film, is it?" said Dad. "My favourite!"

"Your tail's in my ear!" came Theo's voice from behind the sofa.

"What did you say, Max?" asked Mr Black, baffled.

"I said . . . you can't fail to see from here," gabbled Max, quickly sitting down next to his dad. "Best seats in the cinema."

At that moment Ben Magnifico was set upon by an army of peculiar stony creatures. The audience's eyes grew wide and even Jessica fell silent. The boys exchanged a horrified look.

They were sunk. Humans had seen that the gargoylz were alive. Their secret had been discovered.

Max's dad let out a slow breath. "I don't believe it!" he said.

"We can explain," said Max quickly.

"Can we?" muttered Ben under his breath.

"Think of something, Agent Neal," hissed Max.

"My brain's seized up, Agent Black!"

Ben whispered back.

"Those special effects were great," said Max's mum. "If I didn't know better I'd have said those aliens were alive. Well done, boys."

Max and Ben beamed at each other.

"A narrow escape," whispered Ben.

But Jessica suddenly jumped up and pointed at the screen. The fight was over and Toby had popped up with his clapperboard. "I've seen that monkey-faced one before!" she exclaimed.

Max felt as if ice cubes were sliding down his back. Had Jessica remembered the time she'd seen the gargoylz in the garden and Max had pretended they were statues? Or the day she'd caught Toby in the kitchen sink? What were they going to do?

Max gulped, but before he could think of an answer Barry Price appeared on the film, balancing on the churchyard wall.

"I've definitely seen him before!" shrieked Jessica. She burst out laughing.

"Phew!" gasped Max. "She's forgotten about Toby."

"Saved by The Basher!" whispered Ben.

Mum, Dad and Jessica clapped loudly as the aliens finally waved goodbye to Ben Magnifico at the end of the movie.

"That was really impressive, boys," said Mum. "I can't give you an Oscar, but how about chocolate-chip ice cream with sprinkles and flakes?" She ushered Jessica and Dad out to the kitchen.

"Awesome, thank you," shouted Max. "We'll be along in a minute."

"What about the gargoylz?" asked Ben. "How can we get them some ice cream?"

There was a loud burp from behind the sofa and their stony friends waddled out.

Barney looked inside the empty bowl on the coffee table. "Don't worry about us," he said, rubbing his tummy. "We're full up!"

Azzan grinned. "We could win one of those Hollywood prize thingyz for popcorn eating. You know – an Otter."

"You've got it wrong!" said Rufus.

"It's an Octopus."

"You mean an Ostrich," said Toby. "I should know. I saw it on Max's . . ."

Still arguing, they clambered out of the window to make their way back to the church.

"We've just had our first movie screening," said Max.

He waved goodbye to the gargoylz. "And there's only one way to celebrate that."

"Chocolate-chip ice cream!" yelled Ben.

"With sprinkles and flakes!" Max agreed.

4. Barry Saves the Show

It was Monday morning, and Max and Ben were in school. They were supposed to be writing a diary about their weekend.

"I don't know why we've got to do this," complained Max as they hunched over their English books.

"Miss Bleet's just being nosy," answered Ben. "Though I reckon she'll be dead impressed when she reads we've made a movie."

"Our film's loads better than the one Mum took Jessica to see," said Max. "Jess said it was boring."

"I've thought of a brilliant plan, Agent Black," said Ben. "Our movie's the best, right?"

"Right!" agreed Max eagerly.

"And kids pay to see rubbish films, don't they?"

"They do."

"So they'll jump at the chance of paying to see our fantastic movie!"

"Awesome, Agent Neal!" declared Max. "Let's face it – *Attack of the Alien Gargoylz* is the best movie in the history of best movies!"

"So we'll do a public screening here in school," said Ben.

"Public *screaming*, you mean," put in Max, "when the audience sees The Basher's face in close-up!"

"And no one will know that the gargoylz are real," added Ben, "now we've tested it out on your family."

"I bet we'll be let off doing our diaries," said Max, "as we've already worked so hard filming and editing."

"Max Black and Ben Neal," came a weedy voice behind them.

Max's spy radar told him what that meant: short and dumpy, limp brown hair, wobbly eyebrows. It was Enemy Agent Miss Bleet, codename: Wimpy Teacher.

"You're supposed to be writing about what you did at the weekend," sighed Miss Bleet, "not jumping up and down in your seats and whispering."

"We were talking about what we did at the weekend, miss," insisted Ben.

Their teacher looked doubtful.

"We really were," said Max truthfully. "It was so exciting we just couldn't keep still."

"We made a movie," Ben burst out. "And we've brought it in. Could we show it in here at lunch time?"

Miss Bleet brightened up. "What a good idea!" she exclaimed. "I'll watch it too. What's it called?"

"*Attack of the Alien Garg*—" began Ben.

Max kicked him on the shin.

"*Attack of the Aliens*, I mean," said Ben hurriedly, rubbing his leg.

Miss Bleet beamed. "I'm so glad you boys don't spend all your time playing silly tricks."

"Not us," said Max, as if aghast at the thought.

"But meanwhile you can write a nice long entry all about how you made your film," added their teacher.

Max and Ben groaned and picked up their pens.

As soon as the bell went for playtime, the boys raced out to the churchyard wall to tell the gargoylz their plan.

They spotted Toby waving his clapperboard importantly, and Neb pretending to film a row of grinning gargoylz who were galloping about on a gravestone.

"Greetingz!" called Toby, flying up to the wall.

"We're practising for our next movie," explained Jelly. "It's going to be about cowboyz."

"Cool!" said Ben, watching Azzan as he rode around on Rufus's back, waving a lasso.

"But in the meantime, we've got great news," said Max. "Our teacher says we can show *Attack of the Alien Gargoylz* in school."

The gargoylz looked worried.

"But what if those humanz realize we're alive?" said Barney nervously. His eyes began to glaze over. Barney sometimes let out an accidental bottom burp when he was scared. Max could see one coming.

"Don't worry," he said quickly. "If anyone's curious we'll just tell them you're special effects."

"That's OK then," declared Neb. "We'll watch from the window."

"We're going to be film stars!" growled Rufus proudly.

"We've decided to charge everyone fifty p to watch the film," added Ben.

"Dangling drainpipes," declared Toby. "We'll be rich!"

"What shall we spend all the money on?" asked Azzan.

"That's simple," said Max with a grin. "Yummy treats."

"Cookiez and cakes! Cookiez and cakes!" chanted Zack, bouncing around the churchyard.

"We'd better be off," said Max. "We have to tell everyone about the film."

"That's called publicity," said Toby. "I know all about that. I saw a programme on—"

"Oi! You two," came a gruff voice.

Max and Ben spun round.

The Basher was stomping towards them, fists clenched. The gargoylz fled instantly.

"What have we done?" sighed Ben.

"Nothing," growled Barry. "And that's the trouble. You haven't let me see my movie." He poked Max in the ribs. "You said you would."

Max and Ben grinned with relief.

"You're in luck," said Max. "There's going to be a special showing . . ."

"Especially for you," put in Ben.

"In our classroom at lunch time," said Max.

"We thought we'd tell everyone else too," added Ben.

"So they can see what a great actor you are," finished Max.

"I'm looking forward to it," said Barry. He stomped off, smirking horribly.

"That was a close shave!" exclaimed Ben when he was out of earshot.

"We're lucky we've got lightning-speed superspy brains," said Max, "or The Basher might have bashed us."

"But what's going to happen when he sees himself as a stinky alien?" said Ben in alarm.

"Uh-oh," said Max. "We hadn't thought of that."

Ben gulped. "He's going to explode! We'll have to make a quick getaway, Agent Black."

"But at least we'll have made lots of money," said Max, rubbing his hands together. "Let's tell our class about the movie."

* * *

After lunch Max and Ben dashed back to their classroom to get everything ready for the film. They attached Max's camera to Miss Bleet's laptop and then pulled down the blackout blinds, making sure they left a little gap underneath so the gargoylz could see in through the window.

"Roll up, roll up!" cried Max, flinging open the classroom door. "Get ready for the greatest entertainment of your lives."

He was astonished to see a long queue of children snaking down the corridor, all waiting for the grand showing of *Attack of the Aliens*.

Ben collected the money in a pencil pot as the audience filed in.

"Our whole class has come – and the rest of the year," said Max in delight.

Soon the room was full to bursting with jostling pupils, squashed onto chairs and into corners. Barry barged into the room, refused to pay and took over a whole table in the front row.

Miss Bleet popped her head round the door. "Do make a start," she told the boys. "I'll be along in a moment."

Max stood up and raised a hand for silence. "Ladies and gentlemen!" he announced. "Welcome to our cinema. As you're all in your seats, we present for your delight—"

"I haven't got a seat," came a whiny voice from the back of the room, "so I shouldn't have to pay."

Max tuned in his radar: pale, skinny, face like a sour grape. He knew what that meant. It was Enemy Agent Lucinda Tellingly, codename: Bossy Boots. She was standing in the corner, squashed up against the gerbil cage and looking very cross.

"You should have got here earlier," said Max. "Ladies and gentlemen—"

"Anyway, it's not a proper cinema," piped up Lucinda's friend Tiffany. "There's no popcorn."

"You can't have popcorn," said Max.

"It's not allowed."

"Why not?" demanded Lucinda.

"Er . . ."

"Health and safety," Ben put in.

"And I bet you haven't got any adverts," said Tiffany.

"Well, no . . ." admitted Max.

The audience started muttering and demanding their money back.

"This isn't going according to plan, Agent Black," whispered Ben.

Crash! Barry jumped to his feet, knocking several children off their chairs. "Everyone shut up!" he bellowed at the audience.

Everyone shut up.

"You will watch this film starring the great Barry Price and enjoy it, or else," he threatened. He shot a venomous look at the boys. "Start the movie!"

"The Basher doesn't know it," Max whispered, "but that's the second time he's got us and our film out of trouble."

"I never thought I'd say this," Ben whispered back, "but I'm glad he's here."

"Even if he thumps us when he's seen the film," muttered Max, pressing the PLAY button.

At that moment Miss Bleet scuttled in and sat down facing the screen.

The first image focused on some alphabet bricks made into the words BLACK AND NEAL PRODUCTIONS.

The audience tittered as Ben's drawing of the rocket wobbled into the air, but soon gasped in amazement when they saw the flames underneath it. By the time the astronaut was set upon by a throng of weird-looking aliens, they were agog.

"How did you do that?" called Gavin.

"They look real!" gasped Duncan.

"It's all special effects," said Max quickly.

"Animatronics," added Ben.

"Gargoylematronics!" whispered Max. He checked the window and nudged Ben. They could see a row of mischievous eyes peering in.

And then The Basher appeared on the screen and the voiceover introduced Barry the Bashgroozle, the nastiest, stinkiest alien in the universe.

Max and Ben gulped. Barry was going

red with rage to the tips of his big bulbous ears and everyone was roaring with laughter at his antics onscreen.

When the movie was over the audience broke into a storm of applause. The boys hardly heard it. They just wanted to escape from the classroom before Barry could get hold of them.

But there was no chance. Miss Bleet stood up. "Well done, Max and Ben. That was a clever film." Then she turned to The

Basher. "What a brilliant performance, Barry!" she exclaimed. "You're a natural comedian. I have never laughed so much in my life. Let's hear it for Max, Ben and Barry." She began to clap enthusiastically and the whole audience joined in.

For a moment Barry scowled. Then, as the applause grew, a huge, beaming smile slowly spread across his face. "That's me, a natural comedian!" he said proudly, standing up and taking several bows. While Miss Bleet raised the blinds to let the light in, the audience pressed round him for his autograph.

"We got away with it!" whispered Max.

"And got ourselves a pot of money," Ben whispered back.

There was a sudden piercing scream that made everyone spin round. Lucinda was staring out of the window, white with terror. Max and Ben caught sight of the tip of Toby's stony tail disappearing onto the staffroom roof.

"We're being invaded!" shrieked Lucinda. "I've just seen one of those aliens!"

Everyone laughed and Lucinda gave a furious scowl.

"You're imagining it," said Miss Bleet. "They were just puppets on the screen, Lucinda. Although how Max and Ben made them move I'll never know." She turned to the boys with a questioning look.

"Trade secret, miss," said Max quickly.

"Well, it was marvellous, boys," said Miss Bleet. She noticed the pot of fifty pence pieces. "And you've made some money for the class charity."

"No, miss—" began Ben. But it was too late. Their teacher had tipped the money into the collection box labelled WASPS IN NEED.

Then she turned to them. "And here's an Oscar for your hard work," she said, handing them each a gingerbread man.

"Awesome!" they yelled.

Lunch time play wasn't quite over so

the boys ran outside to find the gargoylz.

"Miss Bleet took our cash," said Max as their stony friends jumped up onto the churchyard wall. "But she gave us these instead. Gingerbread Oscars! There's a bit for everyone."

"Cookiez!" declared Zack, running

around excitedly.

"It's ever so jolly being film starz," said Jelly, tucking into the delicious treat.

"I haven't had so much fun since Neb pinned a TICKLE ME sign on the vicar's back," said Toby.

"He couldn't stop giggling for dayz."

"I hope we're going to make another movie soon," said Azzan eagerly.

"We certainly will," declared Max.

The gargoylz leaped about and cheered loudly.

"And I know just what to call it," said Toby. "*Return of the Alien Gargoylz*."

"*Return of the Alien Cowboyz*," said Azzan.

"Alien Skeletonz!"

"Alien Dinosaurz!

"They all sound awesome!" laughed Ben. He rubbed his bruises. "But whatever it's called, I'm definitely wearing armour next time."

Gargoylz Fact File

Full name: Tobias the Third

Known as: Toby

Special Power: Flying

Likes: All kinds of pranks and mischief – especially playing jokes on the vicar

Dislikes: Mrs Hogsbottom, garden gnomes

Full name: Barnabas

Known as: Barney

Special Power: Making big stinks!

Likes: Cookiez

Dislikes: Being surprised by humanz

Full name: Eli

Special Power: Turning into a grass snake

Likes: Sssports Day, Ssslithering

Dislikes: Ssscary ssstories

Full name: Theophilus

Known as: Theo

Special Power: Turning into a ferocious tiger (well, tabby kitten!)

Likes: Sunny spots and cosy places

Dislikes: Rain

Full name: Bartholomew

Known as: Bart

Special Power: Burping spiders

Likes: Being grumpy

Dislikes: Being told to cheer up

Full name: Nebuchadnezzar

Known as: Neb

Special Power: Changing colour to match his background

Likes: Snorkelling

Dislikes: Anyone treading on his tail

Full name: Zackary

Known as: Zack

Special Power: Making himself invisible to humanz

Likes: Bouncing around, eating bramblz, thistlz, and anything with pricklz!

Dislikes: Keeping still

Name: Azzan

Special Power: Breathing fire

Likes: Surprises

Dislikes: Smoke going up his nose and making him sneeze

Full name: Jehieli

Known as: Jelly

Special Power: Turning to jelly

Likes: Having friendz to play with

Dislikes: Bulliez and spoilsports

Name: Ira

Special Power: Making it rain

Likes: Making humanz walk the plank

Dislikes: Being bored

Name: Cyrus

Special Power: Singing lullabies to send humanz to sleep

Likes: Fun dayz out

Dislikes: Snoring

Name: Rufus

Special Power: Turning into a skeleton

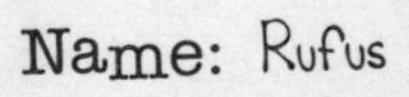

Likes: Playing spooky tricks

Dislikes: Squeezing into small spaces